Alternate Routes

An Alcohol Diversion Program

FAMILY GUIDE

Laura Burney Nissen, Ph.D., M.S.W.

HAZELDEN®

Hazelden
Center City, Minnesota 55012-0176

1-800-328-9000
1-651-213-4590 (Fax)
www.hazelden.org

ISBN: 1-56838-875-6

06 05 04 03 02   6 5 4 3 2 1

Cover design by Theresa Gedig
Interior design by David Spohn
Typesetting by Tursso Companies

Contents

Introduction

Raising kids is one of the biggest challenges of life! Adolescence is a notoriously challenging time in the life of every family. Youth are building their own lives as young adults, and families are watching—ever aware of both the opportunities and risks that await them. Contemporary data suggest that alcohol use among youth remains unacceptably high across the United States and that alcohol is related to many youth problems, including drunk driving, violence, and poor performance in school. Diversion programs have developed as a response to these trends. They have become an important tool in building an "alternate route" from problems to success.

The purpose of this program is to help adolescents understand the dangers associated with alcohol use and to discourage alcohol-related behaviors. It also seeks to encourage healthy growth and development by helping youth to discover personal resources and strengthen a positive direction for their lives. As the parent of a child in diversion, you are part of the success of this program. Even if your adolescent seems distant or difficult, you remain his or her most important guide, coach, disciplinarian, and reference point. The more involved you are, the more likely your adolescent will have long-term success.

A diversion program is not alcohol treatment, but it is designed to be an "early warning system." The truth is that by being here, your child has been identified as being high risk for continuing problems with alcohol and related behaviors.

But there is good news. Intervention or diversion programs have a high rate of success, especially when families get involved. This curriculum is designed to be "family friendly." So get involved, ask questions, and welcome the work of supporting your child to grow into a positive and healthy young adult. There is no more important key to success for your child than your ongoing interest and involvement in his or her life. At every level of your youth's experience, you should feel free to ask questions so that you can understand all of your options and opportunities and plan your own course of action. Your child will not be the only one building an "alternate route," for the diversion experience should always consider families as critical partners.

How the Program Is Organized

Diversion programs across the United States vary somewhat. However, for the most part, a diversion program will engage your child in some type of workshop or group activities designed to interrupt a progression from beginning use of alcohol to more serious levels. An effective diversion program recognizes young people's strengths, acknowledges their challenges, and seeks to support them to make better choices about the direction of their lives. You will likely be asked to participate in a variety of ways. You may be asked to attend family groups, to do homework assignments with your child, or to participate in exercises in family sessions with a facilitator.

This family guide follows the same format as the youth workbook. It is divided into twelve sections and a conclusion, which is called "Your Plan for Success." Each section provides you with a brief summary of the content of the youth workbook, some ideas to think about and questions to consider as family members, and some resources for additional information. Understand that the facilitator of the program is one of your biggest resources and sources of information. Use him or her for answering questions, for guidance, or for information about other local sources of support. While the program is focused on your child's behavior, parents are encouraged to see themselves as very much "in the program" as well. By joining with your child, making your support for the experience clear, and regularly checking in with him or her regarding progress and feelings, you demonstrate how to take a crisis and turn it into an opportunity. Model your willingness to learn, to grow, and to improve your own skills as a parent during this challenging time—and your child will see your courage, commitment, and concern. When possible, try to meet other families who are engaged in the program. You will find that you have the potential to serve as great supports to one another.

1. Changes

- What change is all about
- Changing your own life
- Skills for changing

Starting Out with a Focus on Change

The word "change" helps us to remember that adolescence involves a powerful transition from childhood to adulthood. Even before your child entered this diversion program, he or she was entering a stage of life more demanding and complicated than any other he or she has yet experienced. Only the changes in the first two years of life compare in terms of intensity and rate of development. Adolescence is exciting, fun, and exhausting for everyone involved. Almost every adolescent experiences consequences for testing his or her limits. Hopefully, this diversion program will allow you to examine alcohol use as an unproductive and inappropriate behavior for your child.

While no parent wants to label a child as "alcoholic" (and such a label should be avoided when dealing with young people), it is equally important for parents not to minimize drinking as "just the way kids are today." Alcohol use, alcohol-related legal charges, and the potential for other alcohol problems are *serious* and should be regarded so by everyone involved. Show your concern and give focus and attention to this issue. Your ability to communicate clearly is very important to the success of your child in the program. But understand that your child's alcohol use is typically directly related to the pressures, curiosities, and opportunities of growing up. Adolescents are exploring a whole new world—and alcohol has become part of this exploration. As our communities have come to recognize that adolescence and drinking are a potentially deadly combination, diversion programs have been developed to interrupt these behaviors, to help youth think about the choices they make in their own lives, and to increase their skills for taking their own direction.

Change is the hallmark of adolescence. Most people simply change and grow. They don't think about the process of changing or the power that comes with knowing how to change intentionally. This program, however, provides your child with a chance to learn how to take control of his or her changes and to choose the young adult he or she wishes to become. The program can support growth toward a positive and healthy adulthood by giving the youth extra time and attention in learning important lessons about how to build the life they want.

As a parent, you are most often at the front line of this change experience. You watch your child explore such things as personal competencies; connectedness to you, friends, and the world; feelings about his or her control over the world; and his or her identity. Talk to your child about progress and setbacks in these areas. Remember that no matter how independent your child may seem, you continue to represent essential security. Get to know the person your child is changing into. You may be surprised to learn about a host of new developments!

The Teachable Moment and Time Together

Because of the diversion experience, you (and the courts) have your adolescent's attention. What will you do with it? Parents are encouraged to view themselves as partners with the program's staff in maximizing the important lessons of this curriculum. This section helps youth to understand that change is important, that change is their job, and that they have a say about the person they will change into. These are all critical lessons with which to begin their diversion experience. Parents are encouraged to set aside time with their child this week—and every week—to touch base about the section's lessons, the opportunities for change their child sees, his or her reaction to change, and what actions (if any) will be taken based on these impressions. Although it can be challenging for family members to juggle schedules in order to find extra time to be together, doing so demonstrates that the diversion program is a priority and sets a positive momentum for—and commitment to—the diversion experience.

Family Changes

Perhaps it is not only the adolescent in diversion who is changing but also your family. Maybe you are facing another family challenge. If so, know that the *Alternates Routes* experience is designed to strengthen and support your child *and* your family. It seeks to find and bring out the best of your family life. Contemporary families are under extraordinary pressure. Finances, relationships, health, and emotions all compete for attention and time. Every family goes through times when stresses exceed a parent's ability to cope and when the challenges seem to get the best of us. If you are feeling overwhelmed by the challenges in your life, you might ask your diversion staff person or another support person to help you learn ways of handling the challenges you face. You need not feel embarrassed. Everyone in your family can benefit from your willingness to take care of yourself. You can show other family members the power of asking for and getting help when you need it.

Wrap Up

Be aware of this dynamic time of change in your child's life.

Be sensitive to your child's need to explore his or her world, but remember that you are still his or her primary reference point for right and wrong, as well as for security.

Set aside time together to talk and review progress and setbacks. Remember to use this time as a series of teachable moments.

Acknowledge that family changes may be providing additional stress. Don't feel bad about seeking help or support for yourself if you need it. Model the power that comes from getting help and getting better.

2. Identity

- Who you are now
- Gender, race, ethnicity
- What the world sees

Welcome to Adolescence—New Challenges for Family Management

Among the many words that can be used to describe your child, the word "adolescent" probably leads all others. But what is adolescence exactly? Let's talk about some of the basics. Most experts agree that adolescents have four main developmental tasks. Adolescents seek to achieve

- a sense of industry [useful purpose] and competency;
- a feeling of connectedness to others and society;
- a belief in their control over their fate in life; and
- a stable identity.*

These developmental components are influenced most by you as a parent, along with other family members and your child's friends. Your community, culture, and geographic location influence your child's development in a variety of ways.

*T. R. Lewis, *Understanding Youth Development: Promoting Positive Pathways of Growth* (Washington, DC: U.S. Department of Health and Human Services, Administration on Children and Families, 1997), xi.

Other factors include the presence or absence of racism or classism in their lives and access to education and other resources they need for success. Every parent has the challenging job of accentuating the positive elements among these—and protecting their children from those that might impact them negatively. Parenting an adolescent means going through a set of changes and developmental stages as a family as well. No longer are youth as amenable to childhood-oriented activities or family management strategies. Indeed, families have to grow into adolescence every bit as much as the youth themselves. Parents need to balance a youth's need to explore with the continuing need to have boundaries. Every family experiences challenges at this time, and perhaps your family's challenges have landed you in this program. The good news is that most families do negotiate these changes and emerge with relationships intact, but it involves work to learn new skills and support to apply them consistently.

Family management is a term that includes such things as maintaining discipline, setting aside family time, managing conflict, opening up communication, and planning and celebrating family rituals. How satisfied are you with the success you've experienced in these areas? Might your family life benefit from learning methods for improving the quality of your interactions with your adolescent? Throughout this curriculum, you'll be provided with ideas for ways to enhance family communication and time spent together and other key family management components. Take advantage of these experiences. Your chances of success will increase by talking with your diversion counselor about specific events that stump you and by talking with other families about their successes.

Growing into Themselves: Supporting and Encouraging a Healthy Young Adult

Your child will grow up—whether or not you as an adult guide the process. Despite competing influences (and they seem to increase every day), families (and parents in particular) remain an important voice in the developing adolescent's life. As you learn more about adolescence, remember your own experiences as a young person. Think about what you most valued from your own parents or, conversely, what you wished had been different. How have these experiences shaped the kind of parent you are now, during your own child's adolescence? As turbulent as it can sometimes be, remember, too, that adolescence is a powerful and beautiful time of life—full of new experiences, first times, and risks to be explored. Through the sometimes painful experiences of setting limits, applying discipline, and power struggles, parents and youth can lose touch with one another regarding the positive aspects of this stage. Whenever possible, cherish and celebrate this important time in your adolescent's life and communicate your support and dedication to your child through his or her searches and struggles. This section will provide your adolescent with many opportunities to explore this important time. Invite yourself into that process.

Wrap Up

Know the basics of adolescent development. Remember that this is the "heavy-construction" phase of the development of human identity on the way toward adulthood.

Remember that you remain an important and central influence on the choices your child makes. Talk to your child openly about his or her choices and the journey toward adulthood.

Take a look at how satisfied you are with your family management. Be open to learning new strategies.

Look at the numerous resources related to learning about parenting adolescents, and get to know other parents with adolescents. (See the back of this book for a list of print and online resources for families with adolescents.)

3. Responsibility

- Who counts on you and whom you count on
- Hurting others and being hurt—and what to do about it
- Honor and living out of it

Learning about Responsibility

This section focuses on how to help young people become more responsible and accountable. Keep in mind that responsibility and accountability are developmental acquisitions. Older adolescents should be able to handle these ideas better than younger adolescents. Learning to be responsible, learning that our actions have an impact on those around us—including people we know as well as people we may not know—is of critical importance at this time of life.

As children move developmentally from concrete thinking (childhood) to more abstract thinking (adulthood), they are able to consider concepts such as integrity, honor, and loyalty. These all play a role in their sense of accountability. This section assists youth in understanding that a lack of accountability or responsibility is an unacceptable option for young adulthood. It also gives them a deeper understanding of how to grow beyond the freedom from responsibility they experienced in childhood.

Your Role in Your Child's Developing Sense of Accountability

Typically, families of adolescents in a diversion program find themselves *frustrated*. Perhaps you've known for some time that your child was headed for trouble. There may have been experimental drinking episodes, friends you weren't in favor of, or unsuccessful attempts at discipline.

Today, allow yourself a momentary reprieve from this frustration. Take heart in knowing that the diversion program is a step in the right direction, and that you are not alone in your efforts to guide your child toward a more responsible and accountable life. The program staff, this curriculum, and the court's attention have all converged to guide your child toward better decision-making skills. Now begin to think about how you can build accountability and responsibility into your child's life. What is your role in this process?

Do a self-check on the messages that you are sending about your child's responsibilities around the house, at school, and in other environments. How can you strike new balances, forge new agreements, and explore new methods for demonstrating commitment with your child? Keep in mind that adding diversion presents yet another commitment to your child's life.

Also, check your own degree of modeling; are you as conscientious as you'd like to be regarding your own commitments? Are you sending messages that, although your child's commitments are important, you don't follow through on your own? Are there ways that you can demonstrate what follow-through on a commitment means? If so, do it, and talk to your child about the experience.

Be mindful that if following through is not your child's strong suit, your role will remain *primary* in directing him or her to maintain commitments. Talk to your child about his or her frustrations and resistance to following through. Take time to ask questions and truly listen to the responses. Are there adjustments that you can make that don't involve letting go of your parental responsibilities? Are you satisfied with your skills in managing your child's behavior? Are you interested in accessing additional resources that might expand your skills? (See the resources at the end of this book.)

There may be rewards in your child's life that would make keeping commitments worthwhile. Keep in mind that the abstract satisfaction that adults get from being responsible may not be fully developed in youth. In other words, your child may need something concrete such as a special privilege. Even a pat on the back or a hug might be motivating. We all need rewards. How can you reward your child as he or she makes strides in being accountable and responsible?

Wrap Up

Accountability and responsibility are developmental acquisitions. We have to help youth build these behaviors, not merely punish them for the absence of these behaviors.

Be mindful of the messages that you as an adult send to your child about commitments. Do you always follow through as you should?

While your frustration is understandable, realize that the diversion program is here to help you. As much as possible, set aside this frustration and begin to think about how to build a stronger sense of accountability and connection in your child.

Build in rewards where possible. Maintaining commitments and staying accountable can be difficult. We all need a reward.

4. How Alcohol Got You Here

- How alcohol got you here and what you can do about it
- The role of alcohol in your life up until now

Alcohol as a Symptom

There is no doubt that alcohol is the reason that you and your child are involved in a diversion program. Most experts agree that young people need to be aware of the laws regarding alcohol use, the properties of alcohol, and the risks associated with alcohol use in their lives. At the same time, most would also agree that simply learning about the risks and dangers of alcohol isn't enough to grow a healthy and capable young adult. The reality is that ending up in a diversion program is as much a result of poor choices, limited coping capability, and lack of judgment as it is a problem with alcohol.

Much of the *Alternate Routes* curriculum focuses on these underlying aspects. This section specifically focuses on engaging young people in meaningful and open dialogue about how alcohol has interacted with their choices, their friends, and their experiences. There is intentional effort to avoid labeling the youth as "alcoholics." While it is important for youth to know the danger signs of problems with alcohol, it is equally important to avoid unproductive confrontations or power struggles with youth. Terms such as "chemically dependent" or "addicted" are powerful words that should be avoided, unless a youth has been assessed by a licensed professional substance abuse expert who is experienced with adolescents. In fact, this degree of substance abuse is rare in youth. Most young people who explore alcohol do not end up as alcoholics. In reality, the greater dangers of adolescent alcohol use have to do with the traumas associated with intoxication such as car accidents and violence. Although many of these are deemed "accidental," youth need to understand their responsibility for alcohol-related injuries and stresses.

What You Can Do to Promote Alcohol Awareness

Youth are watching their parents, which means that your own attitudes toward alcohol use are worth examining. Without blaming, can you identify the messages that you (or other family members) may have sent to your child regarding the role of alcohol in adult life? Does your child view alcohol as a central feature of celebrations or a means of dealing with anxiety, frustration, loneliness, or pain? Have you talked with your child about alcohol problems that may be present in your own family? Have you been satisfied with the outcomes of these conversations?

If you as a parent are struggling with an alcohol problem, the most important thing you can do for your child's success is to get help. Your diversion counselor can connect you with resources that can support you during this brave decision. If your spouse or another son or daughter in the family has a problem with alcohol, talk frankly with your child about what is happening. Trying to protect the child from the situation is often impossible. Youth frequently know much more than we think they do. Using good judgment, talk with your child about the problem and assure him or her that it is the responsibility of the adults in the family—not the child—to resolve the problem. Help your child find his or her own ways of coping, and talk about the risks associated with using alcohol to address life challenges.

If you are a social drinker, talk with your spouse about your family policy toward alcohol. If you've never had a "family alcohol policy," this might be a good time to consider one. Talk about the appropriateness of serving alcohol at family events. Understand that you are modeling appropriate alcohol use at all times. Underscore the reality that while alcohol use may be all right on a social basis for adults, it is illegal for youth.

Wrap Up

Knowing the risks of alcohol use in adolescence is important. However, a central goal of this program is to help youth understand that alcohol use is often only a symptom of other problems such as poor decision making.

If there is an alcohol problem in your family, get help. Many resources are available.

Be aware that you are always modeling appropriate alcohol use. What messages are you sending?

5. Relationships

- The people to whom you are connected
- Old relationships and new ones
- Positive relationships and negative ones
- Skills for improving relationships
- Mapping support and conflict
- Giving and getting help
- Repairing harm: Tools for reaching out

Being Connected to Others—The World of Relationships

No transition in adolescence is as significant as the ways in which your child's relationships will change: to you as a parent, to siblings, to friends, to authority figures in general, and to the community at large. This section asks your child to think seriously about his or her satisfaction with the relationships in his or her life. It underscores the importance of having good relationships with others and introduces skills for building, assessing, deepening, and, when necessary, repairing relationships. It supports the youth in examining whether their relationships are positive or negative and in taking responsibility for changing or ending relationships that aren't positive or healthy.

Families as the Relationship Lab

As the web of relationships expands for young adults, the family remains the place where all the lessons converge. What messages are sent in your family about the importance of relationships? What is the quality of relationships in your family? Do they need to be improved?

As your child explores relationships in this program, take time to talk with him or her about the kinds and quality of relationships in his or her life. Like it or not, alcohol has probably played a role in relationship changes in your child's life. Exploring this is an important part of the diversion process. You may know a lot about your child's relationships, or you may find much that you did not know at all. You are a critical observer and historian of your child's experiences with relationships, and you have many insights to offer.

Because of the diversion experience, your family is also engaged in a new relationship with the juvenile justice system. What does this mean for your family? Has it been discussed? What can you do as a parent to show your child that engaging in honest and authentic relationships with authority figures and professionals is critical to his or her success? Parents who can show a positive mind-set here greatly increase a youth's chances of completing the program successfully.

Wrap Up

Changes in adolescence mean changes in a young person's world of relationships.

Alcohol use has likely had an impact on your child's relationships. Exploring this is important.

Learning skills to start, assess, develop, maintain, and repair relationships is critical for successful young adulthood.

Be mindful of the messages that are sent in your family about formal and informal relationships and their place in life.

Send consistent messages about the importance of honest and authentic relationships with professionals in the juvenile justice system.

6. Your Vision

- Ceilings and doors on hopes and aspirations
- Thinking wide and deep about what is possible
- Making a living, making a life
- How to draw a map of the life you want

Building a Path to the Future: The Role of Aspiration

Your child's future is an open book. He or she has unlimited potential. Yet often, through a variety of ways, children may begin to receive messages that cause them to believe that their options for the future are limited. This program believes that every young person (and family) has greatness inside of him or her. The question is, does the youth's environment promote this greatness or attempt to conceal it? This section asks your child to explore his or her hopes, dreams, and aspirations and examine the extent to which they are present in day-to-day life, activities, relationships, and commitments. Likely, if alcohol is part of your child's life, he or she is not as focused on these things as would be desirable. The goal of this section is to help youth reorient themselves to their aspirations. Youth who are working toward achieving a dream usually find it easier to avoid the kind of short-term satisfaction that drinking may provide.

How to Grow a Vision in an Adolescent

We all had dreams as adolescents at one time—then life happened. Some of us had to leave our aspirations behind—not everyone gets a chance to live out his or her dreams. Some of us fulfilled our deepest aspirations through luck, skill, opportunity, dedication, and hard work. Most of us fall somewhere in the middle.

Still, every parent has hopes for his or her child. Sometimes parents fear that involvement in a diversion program means that a youth is irreparably on the "wrong track." Subtly or overtly, they may begin communicating that the youth can't reach his or her dreams. It is important that through the frustrations and challenges of parenting, through the hassles and complications of diversion, parents avoid sending the message that a youth can't resume a healthy and positive path. Diversion can be a troubling but important "side trip" on a youth's adolescent course—important and positive outcomes can emerge from the process. A youth can emerge with a more realistic, yet no less powerful, vision for his or her life, along with improved and grounded skills for attaining it.

Your child may have been hurt by the loss of a dream or something for which he or she hoped. The loss may have affected him or her so deeply that alcohol use became a temporary anesthetic and distraction. This is important to explore with your child. As a parent, you are in a better position than anyone to notice these more subtle changes.

Have you ever spoken with your child about his or her aspirations and hopes? Take time to explore these ideas with your child, and reinforce your child's belief that he or she is capable of achieving anything with enough commitment, hard work, and dedication.

Be a Role Model

If life forced you to leave a dream behind, you can teach your child the power of an aspiration by rediscovering the greatness inside yourself. What aspiration did you have to set aside? You can revitalize your own life as an adult by rededicating yourself to achieving your dream. If you do this, you will add greatly to your child's understanding of the amazing power that a vision can provide.

Wrap Up

Every adolescent has some kind of vision in life. Maintaining a vision through the journey of adolescence is challenging.

Having a vision is an important motivator and reference point for every healthy person.

Be mindful of the messages you send about your child's ability to accomplish his or her aspirations. Stress the need for skills and hard work to attain a dream.

Carefully watch to see if the loss of a vision has contributed to problems with alcohol.

Explore your adolescent's aspirations, and reinforce the idea that he or she has greatness inside of him or her.

Show your child the power of a dream by reconnecting with a goal or pursuit that you have neglected.

7. Reaching

- Risking different ways of being in the world
- Experimenting
- Exploring
- Facing fears

Normally, adolescents are natural risk takers. They tend to take a lot of chances and receive a variety of lessons from the "school of hard knocks." Some youth require more lessons in risk taking than others. Often, youth in diversion have associated alcohol with other types of risk-taking behaviors.

But despite the dangers associated with certain types of risk taking, healthy risk taking is an important part of life. Every successful adult has had to learn to assess opportunities and take calculated risks that offer benefits and rewards when fulfilled.

This section seeks to help youth explore the differences between various kinds of risks and to learn criteria by which they can make better decisions about whether or not to take a risk. They will explore thoughts, feelings, and experiences with risk taking and compare successful and unsuccessful risk-taking episodes.

The Family Role

As a parent, it can be hard to watch your child take risks that may be perceived as dangerous. Youth may conceal the risks they are taking because they know that their parents' attitudes may be less than positive. But parents have a role in helping youth to think differently about taking dangerous risks. Talking honestly about your knowledge of your child's risk-taking behavior, clearly stating your expectations about refraining from dangerous risk taking, and clearly asserting consequences for exceeding these parental limits are essential to changing youthful behavior from irresponsible risk taking to thoughtful action. Remember, too, that adulthood often involves taking chances that extend beyond one's existing comfort zone. Taking these chances is of vital importance in establishing an adult identity.

Wrap Up

Risk taking is a normal and important part of life. It's essential to distinguish between healthy and unhealthy risk taking.

Parents play a large role in keeping the dialogue open regarding acceptable levels of risk behavior. You are a critical reference point in establishing limits to risk behavior.

Supporting youth in their decisions to take healthy risks is key to the development of a strong young adult identity.

8. Spirituality

- Fuel for living—what is yours?
- Spiritual ways of being in the world
- What you have to be grateful for—appreciating the gifts in your life

Helping Your Child Explore His or Her Spiritual Life

This section seeks to determine if spirituality is an important part of your child's life and, if so, how it might provide energy, hope, and support for the challenges of adolescence. This section does not focus on religion per se, although youth may feel most comfortable talking about spirituality in terms of religion. This section does seek to assist your child in identifying what spirituality means to him or her, what he or she is grateful for, and how to live more spiritually in the world.

Talk with your child about his or her spiritual life. Listen to his or her struggles, searches, and questions about this important aspect of life. Understand that as your child explores so many other aspects of his or her identity and life, he or she may be questioning religious or spiritual ideas. How can you support him or her? How can you communicate your respect for various choices? How can you transmit your own beliefs while demonstrating respect for your child's own spiritual values?

To the extent that spirituality is important to you, you may strongly wish to provide your child with a sturdy spiritual foundation for living. Many youth will wish to incorporate these spiritual principles in their identity. If that is the case with your child, build such dialogue about spirituality into your relationship and find ways to share spiritual experiences. Of particular importance may be gentle exploration of the ways in which alcohol interferes with one's spiritual life and how this can be addressed.

Wrap Up

Spirituality is an important part of many people's lives.

As developing young adults, youth often have many strong questions, feelings, and ideas regarding spirituality.

If spirituality is viewed as an important resource for youth, this can be an important area to explore and support as a family.

If spirituality is an important part of a youth's life, examining the degree to which alcohol use has interfered with spiritual development can be a way to talk about changing alcohol-related behavior.

9. Justice

- Unfairness and justice in the world around you
- Getting involved in making the world a better place
- What one person can do

Thinking about Justice

As youth become more abstract thinkers, they observe the world around them in new ways. They become more interested in the rights of people, especially after learning how various groups have been treated unfairly in the past. They may look around the contemporary world and see ample evidence that unfairness continues to persist despite our efforts to improve in these areas. They developmentally and appropriately should feel a sense of frustration and inquiry about these matters, and their energy, curiosity, and ideas about how to make the world a better place should be encouraged. However, youth also exercise their powers of judgment through this process—often clearly identifying the "unfair" behaviors of others while completely oblivious to ways in which they themselves may be equally unfair.

Youth who have received an alcohol-related citation may become fixated on the idea that they are being treated unfairly in their diversion experience. For example, they may say that a police officer unfairly hassled them or that someone betrayed their confidence. This program doesn't seek to avoid such dialogue. Rather, it seeks to use perceptions of injustice to help young people realize how they contributed to their situation and develop a wider lens with regard to the relative fairness and injustice of the world around them. In other words, one important goal of diversion is to help youth take responsibility for the events that brought them here, rather than blame others for their situation.

This section also underscores the importance of laws regarding alcohol for safe and civil social interactions in public life. It examines these laws from a variety of perspectives, for example, what community life would be like if people could drive drunk.

The reality is that injustice is real, and young people have a realistic need to explore and take action. However, when it comes to the types of charges that occur in diversion, youth often need guidance to explore what is injustice and what is an opportunity to turn their lives in a new direction. In most cases, we ultimately want to cultivate a spirit of gratitude in each youth for the experience of diversion and a recognition that the consequences of their alcohol use could have been far more damaging to themselves, to their family and friends, and to their community than they were. It is important for them to understand and recognize that among the legal consequences for illegal drinking activities, there are others which are far more invasive and serious. In many respects, diversion is a privilege.

Talk with your child about the situation that led to the alcohol-related charge. Urge as much dialogue as possible ' regarding self-responsibility for the situation. Talk about choices, community safety, and the dangers associated with deviating from social norms. Additionally, it can be important to examine your child's role models. Are they abiding by socially accepted rules and norms regarding alcohol use? If not, how can you discuss this openly and honestly?

Wrap Up

Youth are interested in issues of justice and injustice. They may be prone to feeling persecuted by the law as opposed to seeing diversion as an opportunity for change.

Diversion seeks to support youth to accept responsibility while respecting their need to explore injustice.

Talk with your child about laws relating to alcohol use. Check on whether adult role models adhere to those rules and norms.

10. Your Gifts

- What you can do that no one else can do
- What you can do that you're proud of
- Where you want to explore
- What others value in you

Your Child's Gifts

Every child has qualities, abilities, and attributes that can be regarded as gifts. What's more, there will never be another person exactly like your adolescent. Some youth are more knowledgeable than others about their own gifts. Some have benefited from having musical, artistic, or athletic talent recognized and developed. A primary goal of any organized program of support, education, and assistance—including diversion—should be to help each young person identify and explore just what his or her gifts might be.

Just because your child is having a problem doesn't mean that he or she lacks gifts and talents. Indeed, this can be a frustrating dynamic to the parental experience: How could my child do this when he or she has so much going for him or her? Yet, in truth, youth often don't fully realize how special, unique, and irreplaceable they are.

Adolescence is a time of life that frequently strains one's self-esteem. Even the most clearly gifted youth sometimes see themselves as inferior or untalented. Helping youth to realize, appreciate, and apply their talents is an excellent method for motivating them to switch gears from high-risk and unproductive behaviors to low-risk, prosocial, and genuinely productive behaviors.

This section engages your adolescent in a variety of activities for exploring or realizing his or her gifts. As a parent, you can support this process by sharing your ideas about your child's gifts with him or her as well as with the diversion counselor. Consider also whether these gifts are being used in your child's day-to-day life. Are resources or time allocated for music lessons, athletic involvement, or the like? If not, why? Do you need assistance to involve your child in activities that will develop his or her gifts?

Be aware of the power of a gift, a positive skill, or an ability to produce amazing results in anchoring your child in a more positive life course. It is in everyone's best interest to find where strengths exist, reinforce them, and unleash them for the greater good. Your child may have a passion for learning more about an area in which he or she is not particularly gifted. Invest in opportunities for your child to explore these areas as well. Strengths will develop. Reinforce your belief that they exist and are worth looking for.

Wrap Up

Every young person has gifts, but not all young people realize that they have them.

Participating in activities that grow out of a youth's strengths can be a way to redirect a life of unproductivity and irresponsibility into a life of productivity and prosocial action.

Recognize that alcohol may have impacted the degree to which your child has focused on or found his or her gifts.

Although you may be frustrated with your child's alcohol-involved behavior, show your child that you can see his or her gifts and that you believe in him or her.

11. Having Fun

- Thinking about natural highs
- Exploring ways to enjoy your life
- Taking risks in safe ways

Youth Know How to Have Fun

Most youth know how to have fun. Even youth who are troubled often manage to have more fun than many adults. Some youth, however, don't develop the important ability to balance fun with work. They never learn to balance momentary thrill seeking and short-term highs with longer-term commitments and more fulfilling experiences.

Adolescents possess an innate need to have fun. Any program that seeks to change adolescent behavior must balance responsibility with the youth's own version of a good time. This section supports youth to develop their repertoire of stress-relieving, funny, and enjoyable activities that don't involve alcohol. It also discusses the fact that once alcohol becomes part of the "fun equation" it may come to dominate and, over time, eliminate nonalcoholic recreational activities.

Families Having Fun

To grow together as a family, to communicate, to share the love, support, and encouragement of one another as family members, it is essential to spend time together having fun. Take time to talk to your adolescent about ways he or she would like to have more fun together. What activities would he or she like to do as a family? Most adults assume that adolescents would rather have a root canal without anesthesia than hang out with their parents. They might be surprised to learn that most youth report they would like to have more time with their parents and families. Youth suffer as much as anyone from the fast pace of modern life and the loss of quiet time to be together. They may long for simple opportunities to share and laugh and grow in a safe and secure place surrounded by people they feel good about. Can you make more time in your family life for these kinds of things? How can your adolescent assume more leadership in directing the events?

Wrap Up

Youth are natural "good-times" experts. They often know more than the adults around them about how to have fun.

Alcohol use can begin a slow process of edging out nonalcoholic ways to have fun.

Youth need to have fun with family as well as friends.

Take an inventory of your own family profile of fun activities and time together. Increase family fun together, if you can, in ways that are healthy and incorporate your youth's ideas.

12. Staying Focused

- Coping with emotions: anger, frustration, depression, excitement
- Keeping balanced and what to do when you lose your balance
- Dealing with stress
- Fulfilling current commitments
- Exploring immediate plans for action and personal commitment

Keeping a Focus

A diversion program requires a commitment of time and resources that extends beyond a quick fix. Diversion happens gradually over a period of weeks or months. During this time, your child will likely experience a range of feelings, attitudes, and levels of interest in the process. Every young person in the program is likely to experience some ups and downs.

Parents can provide essential support during the diversion experience. They can help their youth deal with the stress of the commitment, frustrations over the process not going fast enough, or anger at having missed various opportunities because of being in diversion. Parents can be vital to helping youth ride through setbacks—being patient but firm about a "no-alcohol-use" policy throughout the experience and limiting contact with youth who cannot make or abide by this commitment. If homework is assigned, parents can oversee its completion. Most important, parents can set a tone of consistent and open dialogue about how the process is coming along—without being overly invasive but allowing the youth some necessary privacy as well.

An important part of this section is supporting youth to learn to negotiate difficult emotions and remain alcohol-free. Difficult feelings will always be part of adolescence—indeed, part of life for everyone. Using alcohol to deal with emotions is not a person's only option.

A New Set of Family Norms

Ideally, the diversion experience has provided multiple opportunities for you to explore new ideas, think about new possibilities, learn new approaches, and build new relationships with families who are navigating a similar course. If you've taken these opportunities to heart, your family life may be a little different than when you began the diversion experience, and perhaps you've seen some improvements. By participating, applying the information, and changing some of your approaches, you've modeled your own variation of keeping the diversion commitment. You've also demonstrated the power of learning and applying new skills to make one's life better.

Wrap Up

Difficult feelings are a part of life. Youth need support in learning to deal with difficult feelings without the use of alcohol.

Setbacks happen. Help your child get back on track when he or she has become distracted or lost.

Family modeling of commitment to the diversion experience is indispensable. Changes or adjustments in family life are invaluable reflections of the program.

Conclusion:
Your Plan for Success

- An alternate route: a map toward a life you want
- Finding the supports you need to get you there

Celebrating and Moving Ahead

In this concluding section, your child completes a plan that summarizes the lessons he or she has learned and describes how these lessons will be put into action. Its completion is cause for great celebration. Indeed, your child and your family have come a long way in learning to take a difficult situation and turn it into a positive one. The "alternate route" has become a reality. Your ongoing attention and investment of time with your child will make continuing success considerably more likely. Your adolescent will complete the plan with the help of his or her diversion facilitator—but bringing the plan home and bringing it to life will become something that you will do as a family.

As you conclude the diversion experience, it can be important to know where to go for follow-up or additional services, should you need them. Talk with your diversion counselor about your concerns for continuing family challenges or your interest in follow-up resources. Though you may not need such a referral, leaving the program with a resource phone number can give you important peace of mind that you won't be heading out the door alone. Support resources and people are out there to help you in the event that you need advice or a reality check. Congratulations on your success as a parent—and good luck as you set out to continue this important work!

Wrap Up

The plan for success puts lessons learned into a practical plan for the future.

Make sure to identify additional resources for follow-up or support should you need them later.

Time for a family celebration!

Congratulations to all!

A Special Note:
When Diversion Isn't Enough

No matter how good the diversion program may be, there are a certain number of youth who have more serious problems underlying their alcohol use. The process and experience of diversion gatherings may reveal more dramatic problems and issues for which adolescents need more serious support and professional attention. More serious alcohol and/or drug problems, child abuse and neglect, mental illness, self-harm or other violence in the youth's life are a few of the difficult problems that a subset of young people are likely to bring to any professional help setting.

As a parent, you should know that if you don't see positive changes in your child's behaviors based on the experiences of the diversion program, if you sense that your child is not engaging in the process, or if you believe your child is getting worse, it is important for you to reach out to your diversion facilitator for support and assistance. He or she may call in additional alcohol or other drug abuse or mental health expertise to conduct a more thorough assessment to identify if a deeper problem exists and if a more intensive level of help might be appropriate. Signs indicating such a need might include the continued use of alcohol in spite of new limits, unusual mood swings including excessive anger or sadness, extreme lack of concentration, unusual levels of argumentativeness or frustration in daily life, lack of interest in activities formerly important to your child, or involvement in other high-risk behaviors.

It is impossible to think that one curriculum, a loving family member, or one good friend could solve these more serious problems. Understand that in these cases, the best thing you can do is to get the right kind of help for your child's need.

Resources for Families: In Print and Online

In Print

Bell, R., et al. *Changing Bodies, Changing Lives: A Book for Teens on Sex and Relationships.* 3d ed. New York: Three Rivers Press, 1998.

Benson, P. L. *All Kids Are Our Kids: What Communities Must Do to Raise Caring and Responsible Children and Adolescents.* San Francisco: Jossey-Bass, 1997.

Biddulph, S. G. *Adolescent Recovery Plan: A Curriculum for Chemical Dependency.* Center City, Minn.: Hazelden, 1999.

Cohen, L. J. *Playful Parenting: A Bold New Way to Nurture Close Connections, Solve Behavior Problems, and Encourage Children's Confidence.* New York: Ballantine Books, 2001.

Curran, D. *Tired of Arguing with Your Kids? Wisdom from Parents Who Have Been There.* Notre Dame, Ind.: Sorin Books, 1999.

Doherty, W. J. *The Intentional Family: Simple Rituals to Strengthen Family Ties.* New York: Avon Books, 1999.

Henderson, N., B. Benard, and N. Sharp-Light, eds. *Resiliency in Action: Practical Ideas for Overcoming Risks and Building Strengths in Youth, Families, and Communities.* San Diego: Resiliency in Action, 1999.

Katz, M. *On Playing a Poor Hand Well: Insights from the Lives of Those Who Have Overcome Childhood Risks and Adversities.* New York: Norton, 1997.

Packer, A. J. *Highs!: Over 150 Ways to Feel Really, Really Good . . . Without Alcohol or Other Drugs.* Minneapolis: Free Spirit Publishing, 2000.

Pruitt, D., ed. *Your Adolescent: Emotional, Behavioral, and Cognitive Development from Early Adolescence through the Teen Years.* New York: HarperCollins, 2000.

Saso, P., and S. Saso. *10 Best Gifts for Your Teen: Raising Teens with Love and Understanding.* Notre Dame, Ind.: Sorin Books, 1999.

Tobias, C. U., and C. Funk. *Bringing Out the Best in Your Child: 80 Ways to Focus on Every Kid's Strengths.* Ann Arbor, Mich.: Servant Publications, 1997.

Online

Community Anti-Drug Coalitions of America
www.cadca.org
This national organization provides a wide variety of resource materials for individuals, groups, and communities to utilize in building community-wide alcohol and drug abuse prevention activities.

Federation of Families for Children's Mental Health
www.ffcmh.org
The Federation of Families Web site is a tremendous resource
of materials, research, links, and other information useful to
families and family-strengthening advocates at all levels.

Family Support America
www.familysupportamerica.org/content/aboutus.htm
Family Support America is a national organization encouraging
family-friendly and family-centered support services throughout all organizations serving youth and their families. It
provides training, conferences, publications, and information.

PREVLINE—Prevention Online
www.health.org
This is one of the premier Web sites for information on
dynamic and ever-changing resources regarding substance
abuse prevention, intervention, and treatment. It contains
special resources for family members seeking information
about how to keep children drug-free or what to do if they
have a family member who needs help. PREVLINE is the
National Clearinghouse for Alcohol and Drug Abuse information for the Substance Abuse and Mental Health Services
Administration (SAMHSA), which is the largest source of
federal publications on all matters related to substance abuse.

About the Author

Laura Burney Nissen, Ph.D., M.S.W., is currently an Associate Professor of Social Work at the Graduate School of Social Work, Portland State University. She is also Director of a national program for The Robert Wood Johnson Foundation entitled "Reclaiming Futures: Building Community Solutions to Substance Abuse and Delinquency." She lives in Portland, Oregon, with her husband, Don, and daughter, Hannah Grace.

Hazelden Publishing and Educational Services is a division of the Hazelden Foundation, a not-for-profit organization. Since 1949, Hazelden has been a leader in promoting the dignity and treatment of people afflicted with the disease of chemical dependency.

The mission of the foundation is to improve the quality of life for individuals, families, and communities by providing a national continuum of information, education, and recovery services that are widely accessible; to advance the field through research and training; and to improve our quality and effectiveness through continuous improvement and innovation.

Stemming from that, the mission of this division is to provide quality information and support to people wherever they may be in their personal journey—from education and early intervention, through treatment and recovery, to personal and spiritual growth.

Although our treatment programs do not necessarily use everything Hazelden publishes, our bibliotherapeutic materials support our mission and the Twelve Step philosophy upon which it is based. We encourage your comments and feedback.

The headquarters of the Hazelden Foundation are in Center City, Minnesota. Additional treatment facilities are located in Chicago, Illinois; New York, New York; Plymouth, Minnesota; St. Paul, Minnesota; and West Palm Beach, Florida. At these sites, we provide a continuum of care for men and women of all ages. Our Plymouth facility is designed specifically for youth and families.

For more information on Hazelden, please call **1-800-257-7800.** Or you may access our World Wide Web site on the Internet at **www.hazelden.org.**